Spirit
RIDING FREE

Reading Adventures

L B

LITTLE, BROWN AND COMPANY
New York Boston

Spirit Riding Free: Meet the PALs originally published
in March 2019 by Little, Brown and Company
Spirit Riding Free: Lucky's Class Contest originally published
in July 2019 by Little, Brown and Company
Spirit Riding Free: Spring Beginnings originally published
in February 2020 by Little, Brown and Company
Spirit Riding Free: A Tricky Halloween originally published
in July 2020 by Little, Brown and Company
Spirit Riding Free: Lucky's Treasure Hunt first published
in August 2020 by Little, Brown and Company

Cover design by Elaine Lopez-Levine.

Little, Brown and Company
Hachette Book Group
1290 Avenue of the Americas, New York, NY 10104
Visit us at LBYR.com

First Bindup Edition: August 2020

Little, Brown and Company is a division of Hachette Book Group, Inc.
The Little, Brown name and logo are trademarks of Hachette Book Group, Inc.

The publisher is not responsible for websites (or their content)
that are not owned by the publisher.

ISBN: 978-0-316-49619-3 (pbk.)

Printed in China

APS

10 9 8 7 6 5 4 3 2 1

OFFICIAL
MARK OF
SPIRIT

Table of Contents

DREAMWORKS

Spirit

RIDING FREE

Meet the PALS

by Jennifer Fox

LITTLE, BROWN AND COMPANY
New York   Boston

Attention, Spirit Riding Free fans!
Look for these words
when you read this book.
Can you spot them all?

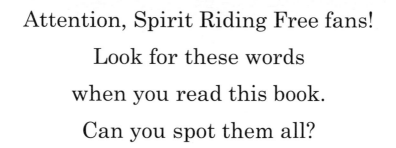

home

friends

ride

horse

Meet Lucky.

She is moving from a big city
to a small town named Miradero.

Lucky

Lucky rides a train to town.

Will she like her new home?

Lucky goes to school.

It is her first day.

She wears a fancy dress.

The other kids give her
funny looks.

Being new is hard.

Lucky has no friends here.

She eats lunch alone.

Soon Lucky makes new friends.
"I am Pru," a girl says.

Pru

"And I am Abigail.
Do you want to come
riding with us?"

Abigail

Pru's dad has a horse ranch.

Pru and Abigail are great riders.

Pru's horse is named
Chica Linda.

Abigail's horse is named
Boomerang.

Lucky likes horses,
but she does not know
how to ride.

Lucky meets a horse
named Spirit.

Spirit is wild.
No one can ride him.

Lucky knows Spirit is special.

"Hey there," she says gently.

Spirit likes Lucky, too.

Spirit lets Lucky ride him.

"Whoa, boy!" she says.

"Slow down!"

Lucky can ride with Pru and Abigail!

Later, Pru's dad says,
"Lucky, Spirit should be yours.
No one else can ride him."

Lucky loves Spirit,
but she cannot keep him.

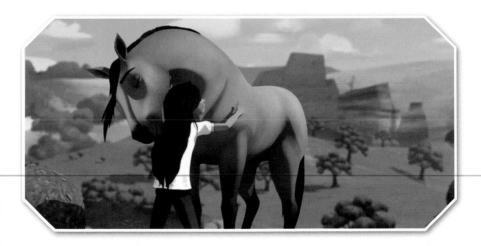

She believes no one can own Spirit
because he is wild at heart.

So Lucky lets Spirit go.

"Goodbye, Spirit.

Be free," says Lucky.

Spirit runs through the hills.

But he is not gone for long!
Spirit loves Lucky and
comes back to her.

Lucky and Spirit can keep riding
with Lucky's new friends.

Together, **Pru**, **Abigail**, and **Lucky**
are the **PAL**s.

Their horses Chica Linda,
Boomerang, and Spirit
are pals, too.

"Come on, PALs!" Lucky calls.

These friends are always ready to ride off on an adventure.

27

Now Miradero feels like home.

There is no place
Lucky would rather be.

Lucky loves being here
with Spirit, riding free!

Lucky's Class Contest

Adapted by Jennifer Fox

LITTLE, BROWN AND COMPANY
New York   Boston

Attention, Spirit Riding Free fans!
Look for these words
when you read this book.
Can you spot them all?

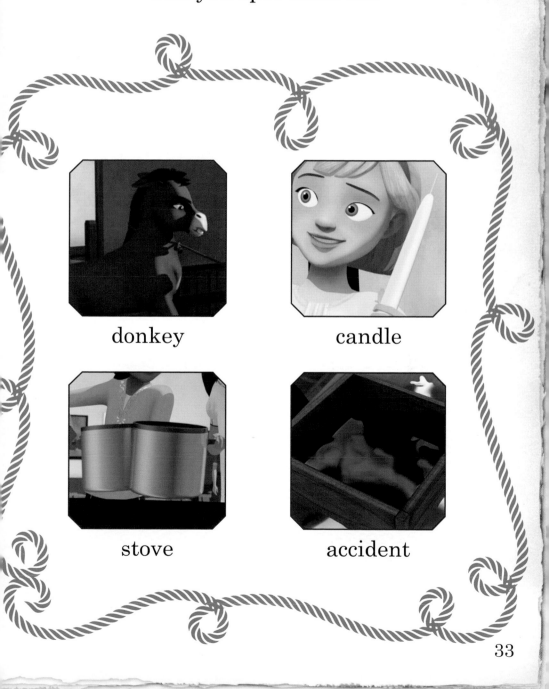

donkey

candle

stove

accident

Lucky runs into the classroom.
She is late to school again!

She arrives just in time
to hear Ms. Flores talk
about a special contest.

"You will work with one
partner to create booths
for our school fundraiser,"
Ms. Flores says.

"The partners who raise the most money will be named the students of the month," continues the teacher.

Lucky wants to partner with one
of her friends, but Pru and Abigail
are already working together.

Lucky needs to find someone
else to be her partner.

Snips says he wants to be partners with Señor Carrots.

Ms. Flores says he cannot do that because Señor Carrots is a donkey.

Ms. Flores asks if Lucky
has found a partner yet.

Lucky does not think she
should work with Snips.

That leaves just Maricela!
"I am so glad we are
finally going to be a
team," she says to Lucky.

Later, Lucky, Abigail, and Pru
talk about the contest.
Lucky hopes she and Maricela
will be students of the month.

Pru and Abigail want
to win the contest, too.
"Ready for a little friendly
competition?" Lucky asks.
"You are on!" Pru replies.

Maricela says they have to work
hard if they want to win.

Lucky would rather ride Spirit
than work on the project.

Lucky goes to Maricela's house.

Maricela and Lucky have the
perfect idea for their booth:
a French café!

Pru and Abigail have
a good idea, too.
"We are making candles,"
Abigail says.

Maricela sees Lucky talking to
Pru and Abigail about the contest.

"Do not talk to them,"
Maricela says to Lucky.
"They are our competition."

The contest is bringing
out the worst in everyone.
Maricela bumps into Abigail
on purpose.

Abigail's horse-shaped
candle breaks!

Pru and Lucky fight for
space at the stove.

Lucky drops her hot chocolate
on the ground!

The night before the fundraiser,
Lucky meets Maricela at the school.
She sees Maricela hiding
Pru and Abigail's candles.

"What are you doing?"
Lucky cries.

Maricela will do anything to win the contest!

Lucky tries to stop Maricela, but the candles fall on the floor and break!

"I have to fix them!"
Lucky shouts.

Lucky stays at the school
all night to fix the candles.

She is so tired that she
accidentally falls asleep!

Uh-oh.
Lucky has forgotten to take
the hot wax off the stove!

The candles melt
into a giant mess!

Ms. Flores wakes Lucky
the next morning.

"Lucky, what happened?"
Ms. Flores asks.

"It was an accident,"
Lucky explains.

Lucky feels awful and goes home.
"Do you think Pru and Abigail
hate me?" Lucky asks Spirit.

Later, Lucky explains
what has happened.
"We do not hate you!" Pru cries.
"You would never ruin our
candles on purpose," Abigail says.

At the fundraiser,
Snips's dunking booth
is everyone's favorite.
He is the student
of the month.

The girls do not win,
but they do not mind.
Nothing beats being
friends forever!

DREAMWORKS

Spirit
RIDING FREE

Spring Beginnings

Adapted by R. J. Cregg

L B

LITTLE, BROWN AND COMPANY
New York   Boston

Attention, Spirit Riding Free fans!
Look for these words
when you read this book.
Can you spot them all?

rears

pregnant

curtsy

waltz

It is springtime in Miradero.
The PALs—Pru, Abigail,
and Lucky—race their
horses across the frontier.

"I will win first
place," Lucky says.
She does!

Their race ends in a valley.

This is where Spirit's herd lives!

The girls walk toward

the wild horses.

A gray horse named Smoke rears
when the PALs reach the herd.

He does not look happy.
He is protecting
something.

The girls see a pregnant mare.
That means the horse is
going to have a baby!

Lucky thinks they should check
on the mare again tomorrow.

Back at Lucky's house,
Aunt Cora has exciting news.

The new governor
is visiting Miradero.
There will be a fancy
ball to welcome him.

All the PALs are invited!
The girls cannot wait to
go to the ball.
They need to get ready.

First, Lucky shows her friends how to be graceful on the stairs. Abigail slips and falls!

Then, Lucky teaches them how to talk to the governor. Pru is so nervous!

The next day, the PALs and
Pru's dad go to the valley.
They will check on
the pregnant mare.

Mr. Granger tries to get to the mare, but Smoke rears at him, too.

Mr. Granger cannot get
close to the mother horse.

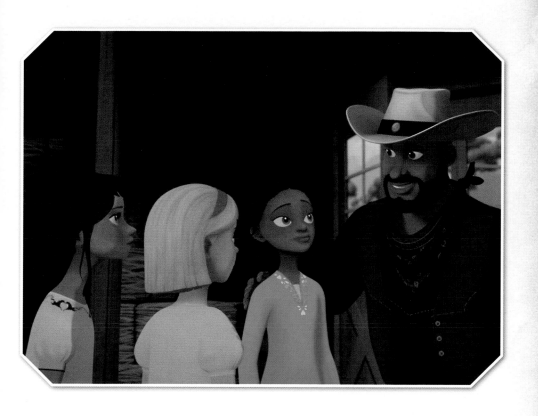

"There is nothing we can do,"
Mr. Granger says.
"She will have her baby
without our help."

Later, the PALs continue
getting ready for the ball.

74

Aunt Cora teaches them how to curtsy.

She also teaches them how to waltz.

The girls are finally ready for the ball!

Just then, Spirit arrives!

He wants Lucky to follow him.

Something is wrong!

"What about the ball?"
Abigail asks.

The horses are more
important than a ball!
The PALs follow Spirit
as fast as they can!

The friends reach the herd.
The wild horses are upset!
"We have to get to the mare,"
says Lucky.

She walks toward the herd,
but Smoke charges at her.

Spirit stops him and guides
the girls to the mare.

Pru goes to the mother horse.
"She is ready to have
the baby," Pru says.

There is no time to
get Mr. Granger.

The PALs have to help
the mare by themselves!

Boomerang, Spirit, and
Chica Linda stand guard.
Abigail keeps the mare calm.

Pru cannot take care
of the foal alone.
She needs Lucky's help!

Pru and Lucky work together.
The foal is born!

Abigail hugs the baby horse.

"He is the cutest thing I
have ever seen!" she says.

The foal takes his first steps.

He falls down.

Spirit helps him up.
They join the
rest of the herd.

The friends are happy that
the mare and foal are okay.
"That little guy needs a name,"
says Pru.

"I have an idea!" says Abigail.

"I bet it is Sprinkles," Pru guesses.

Lucky asks, "Is it Bunny or Gingersnap?"

"I think it should be Governor!"
says Abigail.

The PALs all agree.

Governor is a perfect name.

DREAMWORKS

Spirit

RIDING FREE

A Tricky Halloween

Adapted by Ellie Rose

L B

LITTLE, BROWN AND COMPANY
New York   Boston

Attention, Spirit Riding Free fans!
Look for these words
when you read this book.
Can you spot them all?

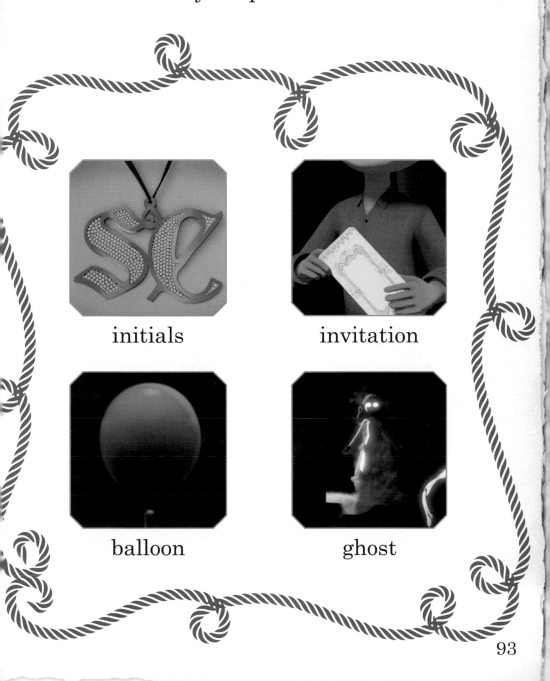

initials

invitation

balloon

ghost

Halloween is very
spooky in Miradero.

Lucky wears a scary mask.

"Boo!" she shouts.

She scares Aunt Cora!

Lucky thinks being scared
on Halloween is fun.

"It is not fun!"
says Abigail.
"Snips scares
me too much!"

Lucky, Pru, and Abigail
want to play a trick on Snips.
It will teach him a lesson.

The PALs have an idea.
The legend of Sadie Crouthers
will help them trick Snips.

Sadie's birthday was on Halloween.
She never had a birthday party.

Her friends were always
too busy trick-or-treating.

Now Sadie's ghost looks
for kids to come to her
birthday party every year!

The PALs tell Snips about Sadie Crouthers.

They even show
him Sadie's necklace.
"What are those
letters?" Snips asks.

"Those are initials," says Lucky.
"They stand for a name,
like Sadie Crouthers."

"Or Señor Carrots!" Snips shouts.
Señor Carrots is his donkey.

Snips wants to give the
necklace to Señor Carrots.

"Sadie's ghost will haunt you if you take the necklace," Pru warns.

Later, Snips takes
the necklace anyway!

He goes to the barn to
give it to Señor Carrots.

The donkey is missing!
There is an invitation
to Sadie's birthday
party in his place.

Snips has to find his donkey!
He runs past Bianca
and Mary Pat.

"A ghost named Sadie
took Señor Carrots," says Snips.
"I am going to her birthday
party to save him!"

"We will give you a ride!" says Bianca.

Meanwhile, Pru and Abigail leave
a trail of carrots and hoofprints.

Snips, Bianca,
and Mary Pat
follow the trail.

It leads them past a creepy
balloon and a bunch of bats.

None of the PALs'
pranks scare Snips!

Soon, Snips and
the twins see
a spooky light.

It leads them to a cake.
It must be Sadie Crouthers's
birthday cake!

"Welcome to my birthday party,"
says a spooky voice.
It is Lucky speaking into a bucket.
Her voice sounds extra creepy!

Now Snips is
really scared!

He puts Sadie's stolen
necklace on the table.

"Take it back!
Just give me Señor Carrots!"
says Snips.

"Promise you will not
scare your sister anymore!"
Lucky says in her ghost voice.

"I promise!"
Snips shouts.
There is a big cloud
of purple smoke.

Señor Carrots appears!
Snips is so happy.

The PALs' plan works!
Snips is scared!

But Lucky wants
to be scared, too.

Just then, the PALs see a ghost horse!
It is pulling a girl in a wagon.

Is it a real ghost?

The girls are scared.

They run away.

"Trick-or-treat!"
someone shouts.

It is Turo and Maricela!

They pranked the PALs!

"Happy Halloween!"

Turo and Maricela say.

It is the best Halloween ever!

RIDING FREE

Lucky's Treasure Hunt

Adapted by Meredith Rusu

LITTLE, BROWN AND COMPANY

New York   Boston

Attention, Spirit Riding Free fans!
Look for these words
when you read this book.
Can you spot them all?

cliff

treasure

skulls

crystals

Lucky is going camping with
her dad, Pru, and Abigail.

This is Lucky's first time camping.
She is excited!

Lucky wants to show her
dad that she is a brave
explorer just like he is.

Mr. Prescott leads the PALs
up a mountain trail.
It is dangerous!

He puts safety ropes
around the horses.

Spirit does not like wearing ropes.

He bumps into the wagon.

It falls over the cliff!

"It is okay," says Mr. Prescott.

"I will get the wagon tomorrow."

That night, the PALs
build a campfire.
Lucky's dad tells
the girls a story.

"I have this treasure map,"
Mr. Prescott says.

"It belonged to a man named Respero.
I never found the treasure."

"Maybe I will find it!" says Lucky.
She wants to go on adventures
like her dad does.

The next day, Mr. Prescott
leaves to get the wagon.

The girls look at
the treasure map.
It has a drawing on it.

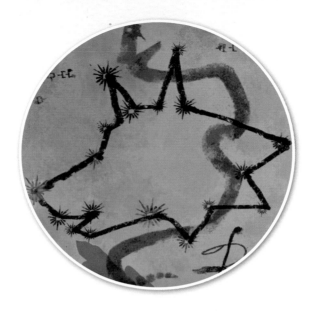

"It looks like a wolf!" Lucky says.

It is a clue.

"We should go to Wolf Ridge!"

Lucky and her friends
ride to Wolf Ridge.
They find another
clue there!

"Some of these rocks have symbols on them. The symbols are also on the map!" says Pru.

"I think we have to follow the rocks that match the map," Abigail says.

The girls reach the end of the path.

Big rocks crash down in front of them!

"That was close!" says Lucky.

"We should keep moving."

"It is getting late," says Abigail.
"Should we go back to camp?"

"Not yet," Lucky replies.
"We must be close to
finding the treasure!"

A cave is at the end of the path.
The PALs hurry inside it
and find a treasure chest.
It is locked!

There are pictures of skulls on the chest.
They look like the skulls on the map.
"I think I know how to open it!"
says Abigail.

She matches the skulls on the
chest to the ones on the map.
The chest unlocks!

Lucky takes a deep breath.

"This is it!" she says.

The PALs open the chest.

It is filled with beautiful crystals!

"Wow!" says Lucky.

"I cannot wait to show my dad!"

Suddenly, the PALs hear
a noise behind them.

It is a growl.

"A bear!" cries Lucky.

"Quick! We have to hide!"

Pru yells.

The PALs hide.

The bear is getting close.

A log crashes down.

It blocks the cave exit.

The girls are trapped!

Meanwhile, Lucky's dad
is looking for the PALs.

He sees Spirit running alone.
Where is Lucky?

Spirit leads Mr. Prescott to the cave.
They have to save the girls!

Spirit pulls a rope to move the log
that is blocking the cave exit.

The PALs escape just in time!

"We are sorry, Dad," says Lucky.

"We were following Respero's map."

"I am just glad
you are all right,"
Lucky's dad says.

The girls tell Mr. Prescott about
how they found Respero's treasure.

They had such a fun adventure!

"You really are turning
into a brave explorer,"
Mr. Prescott tells Lucky.

"I guess it runs in the family,"
Lucky says.
She smiles.

The End

Explore the West and beyond in this original chapter book series!

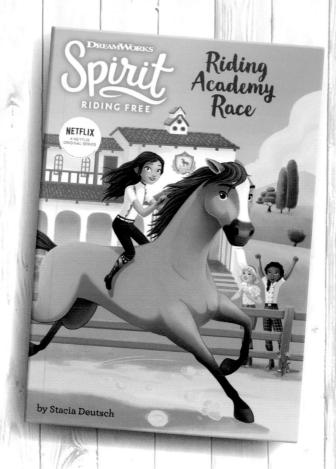

by Stacia Deutsch

Available Wherever Books Are Sold

🎧 Audio Also Available

BOB956

CHECKPOINTS IN THIS BOOK ✔

Meet the PALs

WORD COUNT	GUIDED READING LEVEL	NUMBER OF DOLCH SIGHT WORDS
298	J	62

Lucky's Class Contest

WORD COUNT	GUIDED READING LEVEL	NUMBER OF DOLCH SIGHT WORDS
487	L	76

Spring Beginnings

WORD COUNT	GUIDED READING LEVEL	NUMBER OF DOLCH SIGHT WORDS
487	L	67

A Tricky Halloween

WORD COUNT	GUIDED READING LEVEL	NUMBER OF DOLCH SIGHT WORDS
440	M	73

Lucky's Treasure Hunt

WORD COUNT	GUIDED READING LEVEL	NUMBER OF DOLCH SIGHT WORDS
516	K	65